Best Wishes!

Bonnie Carroll-Marsh
"2010"

Elves on Vacation:
HAVING A BLAST!

Written by: Bonnie Carroll-Marsh

Illustrated by: Michelle Marie Taormina

DEDICATIONS

To: My 2006-2007 Second Grade class at
Long Branch Elementary who inspired this story!
To all of the students, teachers, and staff at L.B.E.

To: Mom and Dad, Del, Natashia, Lizzi, Aaron,
Patrick and Giovanni. You are my JOY!

To: Miss McAuliffe

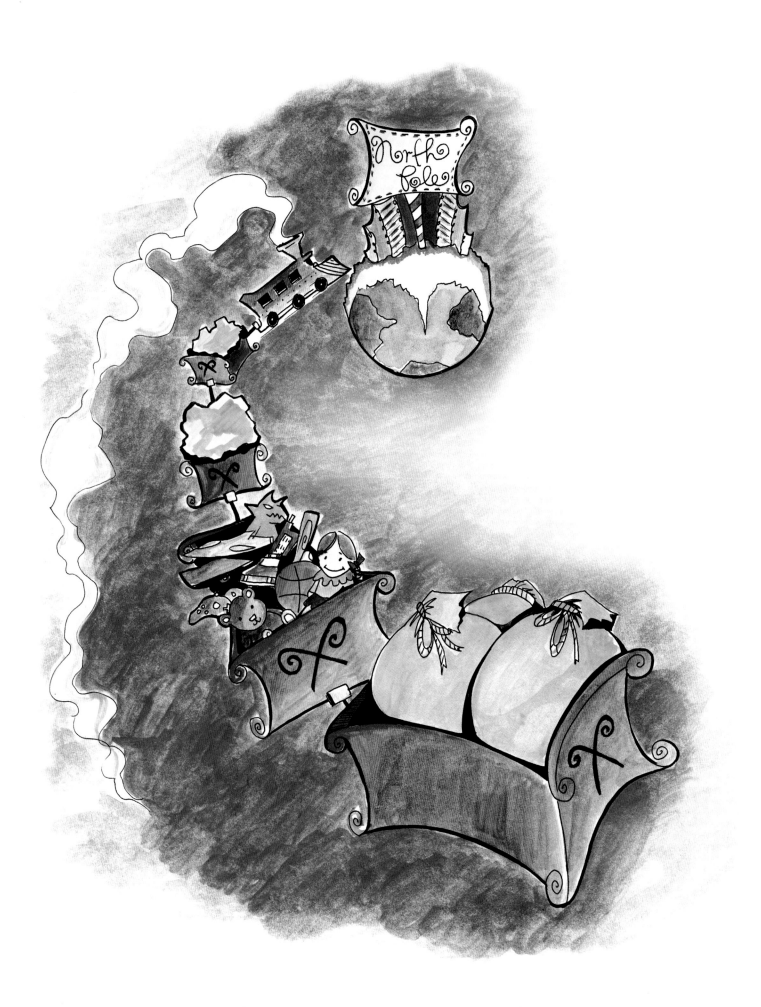

Now, everyone's heard
of Santa's North Pole...
Where Elves build toys
with their hearts and their souls.
The birthplace of Christmas dreams
come to life. Home to Santa
and his lovely wife.

Trinkets, toy trains, race cars and more,
Gidgets and gadgets never seen before.
Open 365 days of the year,
1,000 Elves working as Christmas draws near.

Teddy bears and baby dolls to have and to hold,
and now, the rest of the story that's gone UNTOLD!

Minute by minute, hour by hour
The Elves do everything within their power
to meet the deadline of Christmas Eve,
or Santa's mighty sleigh just won't leave.

Kids' dreams all over the world would be shattered
So, the Elves keep on working like nothing else matters.

Hungry, exhausted and dripping with sweat,
the Elves have done it, their goal is met!
Within the toy shop there comes a great cheer,
the Elves wave goodbye to Santa and his flying reindeer!

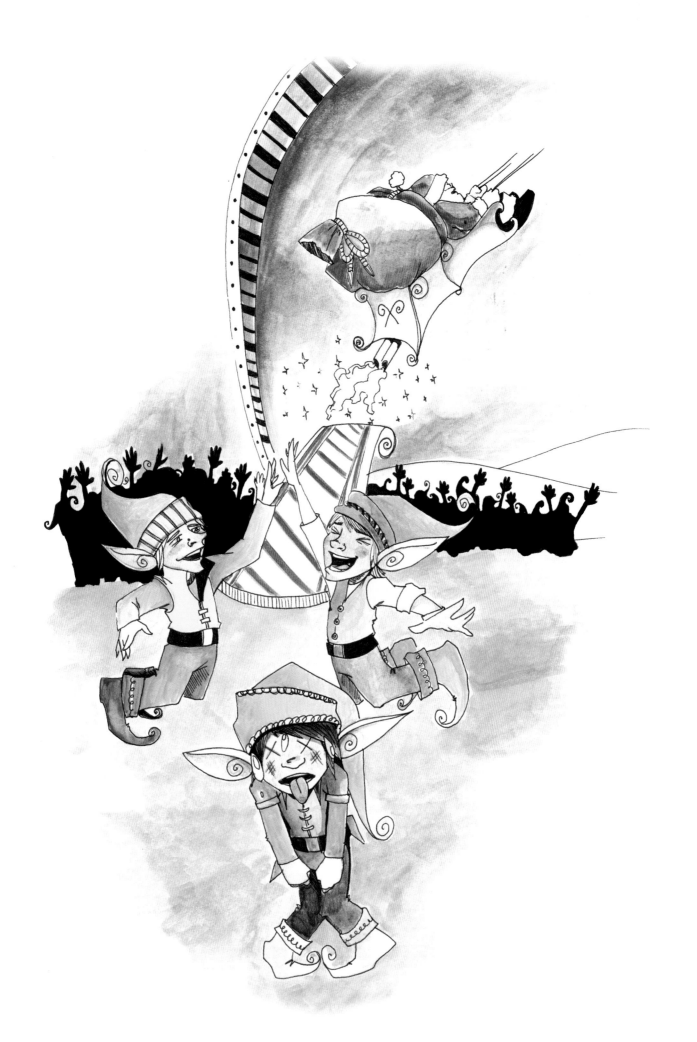

Wait! Who's that? What did you say?

The Elves step aside, they move out of the way.

There on the floor sits little Elf Nore,

who's kicking and screaming,

"I CAN'T TAKE IT ANY MORE!"

"I'VE JUST ABOUT HAD IT UP TO MY EARS!"

His eyes well up, he begins to tear.

"MY ARMS ARE SORE,

AND MY FEET ARE NUMB!

INSTEAD OF THE NAIL, I JUST HIT MY THUMB!

MY EYES ARE BLURRY.

I NEED SOME SLEEP!

Poor Elf Nore begins to weep.

"It's not that I don't LOVE this place…it's just that…it's just…"
Elf Nore begins to plead his case.
"Elves like us are supposed to have FUN,
but we work, and we work with no VACATION!"

"It's time that we all take a little R & R…
go away for a week to places near and far.
Then we'll be refreshed, rested….renewed….
with energy galore!"
The other Elves agreed, they had listened to Nore.

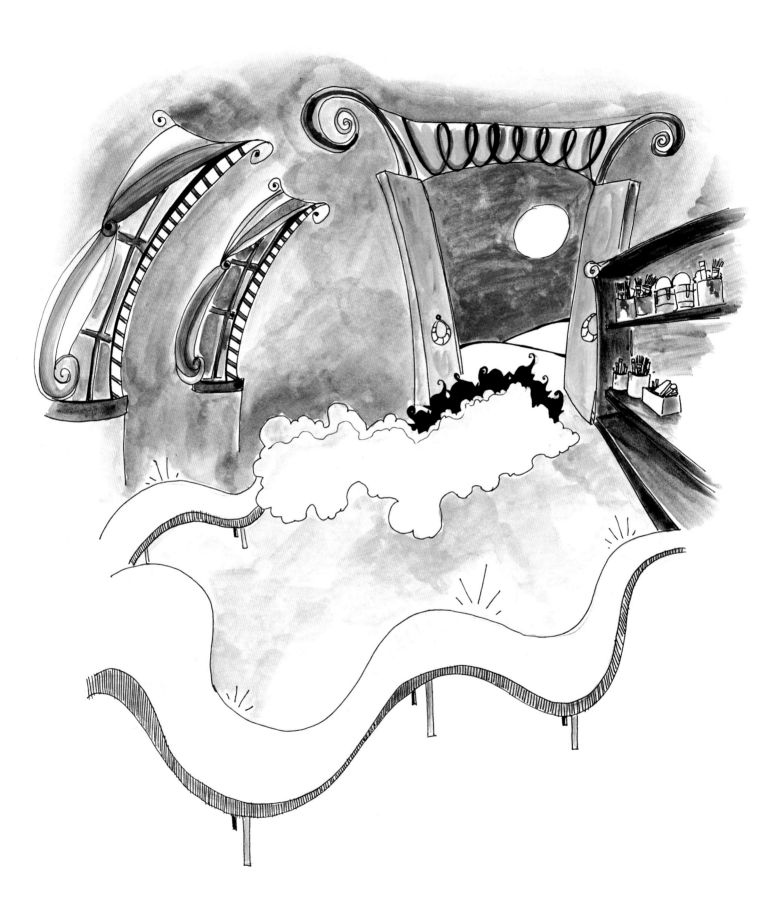

So, they put down their chisels, their hammers and nails.
Rinsed off their paintbrushes, their pallets, and pails.
Unplugged the jigsaws, the routers and drills,
Pulled down all the shades to the windowsills.

They locked all the doors,
and turned off all the lights.
Then 1,000 Elves snuck off in the night.

The Toy Shop sat empty on top of Pole's Peak.
The sign on the door said,
"Be back in a week!"

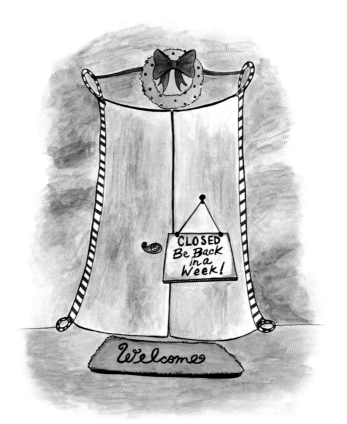

Some traveled by car, onto buses and trains...
While others went by cruise ship, and limos
and jumbo jet planes.

To the "land down under" went athletic Elf Chloe,
who spent a week in Australia boxing with a joey.
One punch, two punches, three punches, four...
Elf Chloe wasn't quick enough.
And so her eye was sore!

ervous Elf Lance spent his time in France,

knowing that this was his very last chance.

to marry his sweetheart, after the dance.

With ring in hand, and on bended knee,

He asked Elf Winnie, "Will you marry me?"

Elf Dina went to China
with her baby sister Amanda,
who wandered off at the zoo
And crawled in with the pandas!

To, "the city that never sleeps" went dancing Elf Kitty,
Doing the latest hip-hop moves in fabulous New York City!
In subway cars and in Central Park,
she kept on dancing 'til way after dark!

Tim and Jim, the identical Elf twins,
went to Antarctica to sled with the penguins.
Over giant bumps and jumps they flew in the air,
and wound up in nothing but their underwear!

On the back of an elephant, rode adventurous Elf Tari.
Who had always dreamed of going on an African safari!
Zebras, giraffes, and lions running free,
From way up here, there was so much to see!

Straight to the boardwalk rushed excited Elf Lil,
who couldn't wait to experience an amazing thrill!
She rode the super sonic, superty-duper,
upside down, quadruple looper!
At speeds of over 100 miles per hour,
Elf Lil shrilled as she zoomed by the tower!

Surfer dude Howie spent his time in Maui,
riding the biggest of waves...
He looked over his shoulder as one rolled over,
and wiped out his best friend Elf Dave!

The rest of the Elves had just as much fun,

or so the newspaper said.

"ELVES ON VACATION: HAVING A BLAST!"

Is what the headlines read!

For the tuckered out Elves,
seven days of bliss had come to an end.
Souvenirs they bought,
Postcards they did send!

Now it was time to get back to Pole's Peak.
After all, it had been an INCREDIBLE week!

Back into cars, onto buses and trains,
Onto cruise ships, and limos, and jumbo jet planes.
Greeted by Santa and Mrs. Claus too,
the Elves returned to work,
with so much to do!

They got down to business as soon as they could,
with joy in their hearts, as all good Elves should.
Laughter and Elf songs flowed through the air,
As toys were created with loving care.

The Elves WERE refreshed, rested, RENEWED!
No one was grumpy, or grumbled, or stewed!
Vacation had given them energy galore!

But, WAIT!
What ever happened to Little Elf Nore?

None of the Elves knew, exactly...
and to Santa, no one could explain.
But the last time they saw him, he was "running with bulls"
down in Pamplona, Spain.

So...,

If you're planning a trip to Santa's North Pole,

you should probably call ahead.

Because you just never know if Santa's Elves

will be on VACATION instead!